The Familiar Process
Prequel to The Green Witch Project
Series
Stacy Rae

Book Cover by Stacy Rae

Illustrations by Stacy Rae

Page Edges and Chapter Page Image by Painted Wings Publishing Services

First Edition 2025

Paperback ISBN: 979-8-9918153-4-5

The Familiar Process is dedicated to my husband Tim. He has been with me from the beginning of this process, and he has even helped me come up with some of the names of characters and locations. A huge thank you to him for never doubting me and not fussing at me because I've chosen to write instead of clean.

Thank you for always being my biggest supporter. I love you.

Contents

Chapter One

August 7, 1890

Luca

"So, Luca Matthews and Colin Jacobs. What services can you offer the GWP?" Atticus Bane rubbed his hand over the newly healed scar above his eye.

"Well, sir, though our powers are only now forming since we turned eighteen, we are already black belts in martial arts and have extensive self-defense training. We've taken numerous classes on potions and charms, and we're ready to help defend those who cannot defend themselves." I stood straight with my hands behind my back, refusing to break eye contact.

"And you're confident this is the position you want at the GWP? Security detail can be rather dangerous." He glanced down at his parchment.

"Yes, sir," I said. "This has been our goal for as long as I can remember."

"Mr. Matthews, I'm aware that your father is a celestial witch. Have you manifested any of these powers yet?" He looked over the rim of his spectacles at me.

"No, sir, not as of our daily training this morning." I glanced at Colin, who slouched against the wingback chair opposite Atticus.

Atticus followed my gaze. "Mr. Jacobs, would you like to add anything?" he asked sarcastically.

Colin shook his head. "No, sir. I think Luca explained it all. We're ready to defend against evil."

Atticus studied him for a moment then looked at the parchment on his desk once more. "Give this to my secretary and report for duty tomorrow at sunrise."

I took the parchment from his outstretched hand and gave a quick nod. "Thank you, sir. We won't let you down."

June 28, 1900

The past ten years went by in a blur. We caught evil creatures all along the East Coast and assisted with transport to take vampires back to Scotland, where they could be dealt with accordingly.

Our powers came in about six months after starting our positions. Colin and I had the power of the senses, which made our sight, smell, taste, hearing, and touch so much more intense. We also learned a few years later that we had the power of clairaudience, meaning we could hear our names being called from over five hundred miles away.

In 1896, Atticus Sr. approached us about stepping into roles as familiars. If we were to be killed, we would be brought back and live as a half human, half animal of our choice. They gave us a week to choose the animals we wanted to become, then we both got tattoos with our silhouette and a cat at our feet. The tattoos had a spell attached so the witch demon could find us in the afterlife. That was the only information we received about the process of changing.

We received word about a rogue warlock causing issues in Salem yesterday. We traveled the fifty-one miles from our post in Shawsville to Salem during the night and met with Atticus Sr. to find out about the warlock first thing in the morning.

Atticus had received numerous reports of the warlock trying to break into the Salem Museum, but by the time the guards got there, he was gone. There were no signs indicating he managed to get in.

Atticus gave me the manifest for the items that the museum had just received to display. I read through the list, and it suddenly made sense why the warlock was trying to gain access. The relics were from a ship that sank in the 1700s. The manifest listed multiple chests full of maps, coins, and jewelry.

One particular piece of jewelry was an amulet belonging to none other than Hazel Craig, a witch who had been killed during the Salem witch trials—a witch who made her name as the evilest spell writer in five centuries. Her spell book left death and destruction across the world before Hector Craig found it in 1755. And the amulet sent for display was said to have Hazel's soul attached to it. If it did in fact prove to hold her soul, it could be just as dangerous as her spell book.

Nearly an hour before sunset, Atticus positioned us behind the museum along the woods, about fifty feet from the back entrance. The residents were told to stay inside and that guards would be watching for a man trying to break in.

The warlock approached just before sunrise the next morning, staying in the building's shadows. We watched for a few moments as he conjured a spell to get inside. Suddenly, a spark shot from his staff, splitting the wooden door in half. He pushed the splintered pieces out of the way and entered the dark building.

We quietly followed him into the museum and watched from a distance. He pulled the string for the lights that led to the storeroom below and paused before starting down the stairs.

Colin alerted the waiting guards in the house next door by lighting a candle and placing it in the window facing the house. We quietly descended the stairs, sticking to the wall to keep the steps from creaking.

The warlock had his back to us when we reached the storeroom door. He had pried open the smallest of the chests and was pulling out the jewelry pieces, looking at each one before tossing them onto the table beside the chest. He placed a small box on the other side of the chest and extracted another. He stared at the wooden case for a moment before opening it and letting out a gasp. He carefully closed the lid and looked into the chest again before slamming it shut and grabbing the small box.

As he turned, we stepped back into the hallway where he couldn't see us. He ran through the doorway, turning as he passed to spew sparks at us from his staff as he ran backward, right into the guards' arms. The second guard ripped the warlock's staff from his grip. The guard holding our prisoner walked him toward us as we got back to our feet from dodging the sparks. I carefully took the wooden boxes from him.

A sinister smile crossed his face. "This isn't over."

Colin grabbed his arm and twisted it behind his back as the guard pulled his other arm back.

"No. It never is," Colin said. "Someone is always trying to steal something from someone else. The cycle never ends."

He snapped the power-blocking cuffs on the warlock's wrists, and we escorted the warlock out of the museum and down the road to the waiting wagon. As I opened the door, the warlock pulled something out of his back pocket. I went to grab it from him, but he dropped it before I could.

Pain radiated through my body, and a bright light filled my vision before everything went black.

Chapter Two

July 2, 1900

Colin

"Colin, it's time to wake up," a familiar voice said in my head.

I stretched and slowly opened my eyes to find myself in the GWP's medical ward. Standing beside me was a tall, skinny black cat. As I attempted to sit up, it seemed as if my body wouldn't bend like it was supposed to.

I looked around the room, but only the cat stood before me. Memories of my last assignment with Luca came flooding into my thoughts. I looked down at my hands, and instead of finding skin, I saw fur. It was gray and very thick.

I turned my head to find the black cat's light-gray eyes. "Luca?" I almost didn't recognize my own voice; it sounded so small.

The cat nodded. "Yes, it's me."

I examined my furry body as best I could. "Our assignment didn't go as planned, did it?"

He shook his head. "No. The warlock pulled out a potion grenade as I was opening the door to the wagon. Killed all five of us."

I replayed the scene in my head. "What happened to the amulet and the other piece he took?"

"The amulet is back in the Craig family's possession. Its box was destroyed, and the chain was melted in one place, but the amulet was still intact. They will keep it safe along with Hazel's other possessions that have been located. The other box he grabbed was completely destroyed. The cleanup crew couldn't even tell what it was."

I looked at the clock on the wall. "How long did it take the witch demon to find us?" I asked before glancing out the window at the sky.

"Today is the second of July. Doctor Mason said we arrived in our cat forms early this morning. I woke up about an hour ago, and he informed me about what happened."

I situated myself into a sitting position. I probably should have paid more attention to how cats moved before I decided to be a cat. It felt like my knees were on backward. Standing carefully, I made my way toward the mirror. "It's gonna take forever to get used to how these bodies work and hearing my voice sounding so small." I tried moving my front and back right paw at the same time and fell over. Standing back up, I moved my front paw forward then my back left paw before switching. I took very slow, alternating steps until I reached the edge of the bed. There, I leaned forward a bit and pushed out and up with my back legs—and promptly toppled headfirst onto the hard floor, my back end slamming into it right after.

Luca gave a little chuckle. "Watch that first jump. It's a dangerous one."

I repositioned myself and sat back on my haunches. At least, I thought that was what they were called. "Let's see you do it, Mr. Know-It-All."

Luca walked to the edge and jumped, landing like he'd been a cat far longer than half a day. He shrugged, or what looked like it would be a cat shrug. "Mason gave me some pointers when I woke up."

I glanced at the door. "Where is the doc?"

"Getting something to eat. He's been here for the last forty-eight hours waiting for us to arrive."

I carefully made my way to the floor-length mirror beside the hallway door to inspect my new form then found Luca in the reflection. "I think I make this look good."

Someone in the hallway chuckled. Doctor Mason came into the room and stared down at me. "I see you finally woke up. I hope you're ready for the process."

My furry brows furrowed. "What process?"

"Your next ten years of training, of course." Mason shoved the last bite of his sandwich into his mouth.

My eyes went wide. "Ten years? Now I know why you don't tell potential familiars very much when we sign up. We know a lot about alchemy and apothecary already. Becoming a familiar can't require ten years' worth of training."

"Let's just get my part out of the way, then we can see how long it takes you. You might be surprised."

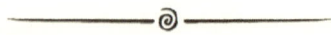

After an intense checkup from Mason, Luca and I were cleared for training. The first thing we worked on was changing from our feline forms to our human ones. It took a lot more energy than I had originally anticipated. We managed to switch forms three times, but after, Luca and I were drained.

Mason said we should regain our energy more quickly over time, and we wouldn't use as much during the change. When we reverted to our human forms the last time, I got to watch the process as Luca changed. The spiritual cloud was almost transparent when we were inside of it, but from the outside looking in, it was opaque and shimmery, swirling with our energy colors.

When it was my turn to switch back to human form, Luca watched me. As my spiritual cloud dissipated completely, I found Luca in awe.

He blinked a couple of times and slowly closed his mouth. "That was more magical from the outside."

Mason handed us each an envelope with our names on the outside. Inside was a piece of paper with a name written in a child's handwriting.

I frowned at the doctor. "What is this?"

He smiled. "Young Atticus was down here with me this morning, and he said he wanted to name you. I told him I couldn't promise that you would accept the names but I would give them to you for consideration."

I turned my paper toward Luca. "Smokey."

He spun his to face me. "Binx."

I smiled at Luca, and he nodded at me.

I turned to Mason. "Please tell young Atticus that we have considered the names and we accept."

Mason lowered his head in acknowledgment. "I'll relay the message. You will need to switch back into your cat forms for at least twenty-four hours every couple of days. You have one year to train before you might be called upon by the underworld, so make sure you're prepared. Tomorrow morning, you need to go see Atticus about your training."

Chapter Three

July 3, 1900

Luca

"Are you aware of how the familiar-binding powers work?" Atticus asked.

"I know they're supposed to help the paranormal, or um… witch we're bound to." Colin ran his hands down his training suit.

Atticus's assistant had brought us our suits last night. We got three brown ones and three gray ones each. We only had to wear them during our ceremony tonight and anytime we were out on assignment.

"That is correct, Colin. You both have the power to persuade and the power to amplify. Do you two want to stay together during your training? We normally allow this as long as you can get along."

Atticus looked over the rims of his spectacles at us, waiting on a reply.

I glanced at Colin then back to Atticus. "Yes, sir. We get along. We're stronger as a unit."

He turned his eyes back to his parchment and dipped his pen into the inkwell. "Very well. We will keep you together as a unit—as you called it. You shall be prompt to any and all engagements and classes until you have completed them. Is that understood?"

"Yes, sir," we said in unison.

"You will earn a salary while you are in training. When you are out in the field on assignment, you will receive a per diem for food and housing. It's yours to keep if you have any remaining. I suggest getting a bank account or utilizing the safes in your bunk rooms here on the GWP grounds while you're training."

"Understood." I shifted my weight from my left foot to my right.

Colin and I had been testing out our feline bodies last night, and I'd landed wrong on my back foot. It was still a bit sore.

"You will meet your trainers and professors this evening at the ceremony. They will give you your schedules. Stop by the library and get your supplies beforehand." Atticus waved his hand as if to dismiss us.

"Thank you, sir," I said as Colin and I turned to leave.

As we sat in our cat forms on the small stage, we listened to the speech Atticus gave the current members. After a few minutes, he turned to me and Colin and introduced us to the crowd as Binx and Smokey. That was our cue to switch back into our human forms, concluding the familiar ceremony.

The members formed a line and congratulated us on our new journey and wished us well in our travels and training.

Young Atticus approached us from the end of the line and wrapped his arms around our waists. "Thank you for accepting the names I wrote down for you. I know you'll do great things with them."

Colin and I smiled down at him and patted the top of his head.

"Thank you for suggesting them. We think they fit perfectly." I ruffled his hair a bit more.

A big smile spread across his face, and he skipped off the stage and down the back hallway. Atticus gave us a nod as he hurried down the hallway after his son.

A group of four members formed at the back of the room. We assumed they were the professors we would be studying under. One by one, they approached us and introduced themselves, then handed us our schedules for the next two years. We had potions, apothecary, combat training, and familiar training.

With the impending workload in hand, we went back to the library to grab journals to keep our notes in. I picked a green leather one, and Colin took a blue. We headed back to our bunks and wrote our schedules on the inside covers so they would be easier to keep track of. We had one week before classes started, so we decided to go back to Shawsville and visit our parents while we could. We packed our bags and headed out to the barn that sat behind the bunk house.

Mason was out there checking on one of the horses. He threw up a hand when he saw us. *"Hello, boys. Headed out?"*

Colin and I flinched, and I raised my hand to my forehead. "Mason, how did you do that?"

He took a step back from the stall door, and a spiritual golden cloud swirled around his body. Once the cloud dissipated, a yellow Labrador stood in his place.

My eyes went wide. "Why did your voice sound like it was in our heads?"

"Because it was. Once you become a familiar, you have the ability to speak to each other telepathically. Once you bind to someone, they can also speak to you the same way."

I furrowed my brows at Colin. "Did you know that?"

Colin shook his head, and I turned back toward the yellow Lab. "That's a good thing, I guess. People might find it weird to know we could talk in our cat form. Not to mention our voices sound so small."

Mason shot us a quick nod. *"Yes, it would be bad if non-paranormals saw a cat talking. It would quickly raise suspicions."*

A smile spread across my face. "I'm looking forward to learning how to talk telepathically."

Colin nudged my arm. "We gotta get on the road if we are going back to Shawsville."

I nodded and turned to Mason. "We'll be back in five days, if anyone comes asking for us."

The yellow Lab bowed his head. *"Safe travels, boys. I'll see you soon."*

I waved and grabbed the saddle off the stand, placing it gently on Grimsley's back. Colin grabbed the saddle from the other side of the barn and lifted it toward Mayo's back. Mayo bucked and moved as far away from Colin as her reins would allow. I watched as Colin tried again to get the saddle on her back before Mayo bucked.

Walking over, I grabbed her reins and placed my hand on the side of her face. "It's okay, Mayo. I'd refuse to be saddled, too, if I had that name."

Colin lifted the saddle a third time and managed to get it in place. He let out a huff. "There is nothing wrong with her name, Luca. She's a horse. She neighs."

"So, you decided to call her Mayo-Neighs Jacobs. She's not a condiment, Colin." I rubbed the sides of the white horse's face. "I don't know why you didn't name her Ghost."

Colin shrugged. "I liked Mayo-Neighs better."

I rolled my eyes and finished cinching the saddle on Grimsley. Then, I grabbed some carrots for the horses and put them in our saddlebags. Taking another carrot, I broke it in half for Mayo and Grimsley while Colin finished cinching Mayo's saddle.

I stood with Mayo while Colin climbed into the saddle, then I mounted Grimsley. Patting Grimsley's neck, I let him know we were ready to go. We started off at a slow trot through the main streets of Salem before we turned to make our way toward Shawsville.

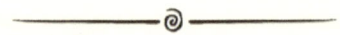

We arrived in Shawsville six hours later and got Mayo and Grimsley into the stables with some hay and water. The hour was late, and our parents would already be in bed, so we stayed in the rooms we rented above the stables.

The next morning, Colin and I left the stables located just a few streets from where our parents lived. Our fathers would already be gone for their workdays, and since our mothers were sisters, we knew they would be having their morning tea on the back porch of one of their houses.

Colin's parents' porch was empty, so we made our way down the path to my parents' back porch. Aunt Lilith squealed when she saw us coming around the corner of the house. She put down her teacup and ran to Colin, giving him a squeeze. My mom peeked out the kitchen door to see what all the noise was about. She gasped when she saw us and came out to give us both a hug.

Vivian, my mother, pulled us up onto the porch and gestured for us to sit. "I'll be right back. I knew I made fresh lemonade this morning for a reason."

"That sounds amazing, Mom. Thank you." I gave her a toothy grin.

"That will definitely hit the spot, Aunt Vivian. Thank you," Colin said as he took off his long-sleeved shirt.

As far as Colin and I were aware, our parents didn't know we had been killed and brought back as familiars. Both of our fathers had been approached with the opportunity to become familiars numerous times, when Colin and I were little, but they had turned down the offer each time. They would never tell us why.

"So, how long are you boys back home?" Aunt Lilith asked as my mom set our drinks on the table.

"We have to be back in Salem in six days to start our training." Colin's gaze shifted from his mom to mine.

My mom's brows furrowed. "What type of training are they giving you this time? I thought you were finished with it all years ago."

I released a long sigh. "Familiar training."

My mom's eyes went wide, and Aunt Lilith gasped, her eyes dropping to her teacup.

"Oh dear," my mom said. "What happened? How did you get to this point? No one contacted us about your deaths."

Tears welled in her eyes as I met her gaze. "A warlock was trying to break into the museum to get some artifacts that had just been discovered on a sunken ship. We apprehended him without incident, but as we were loading him into the wagon, he pulled out a potion grenade and dropped it before I realized he had something in his pocket. It killed all five of us instantly. We were brought back a few days ago."

"You do realize that your fathers won't be happy about this, right?" Aunt Lilith wiped the tear rolling down her cheek.

"I assumed as much, but they never gave us a reason why they wouldn't take the offer. So when we were given the chance, we jumped on it, and I'm glad we did."

We sat and talked about some of our missions that our moms didn't know about then went out and fed the cows, chickens, ducks, and horses for them so our mothers could relax for the day.

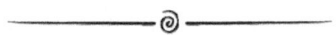

Our fathers arrived home at six that evening and seemed happy to see us. Colin and I knew it would be short-lived due to the news of us becoming familiars. Our moms had asked us to not mention anything until after dinner, so Colin and I made small talk with them until we went out to the porch while our moms cleaned up the dishes. Colin and I sat across from them with our backs toward the yard.

I took a long, deep breath and slowly let it out before making eye contact with my dad, Charles. "So, we get to start training again when we go back to Salem next week." My brows rose as I waited for his reaction.

"That's wonderful, son. What new post are they giving you?" he replied.

"We'll be training new witches," I said, dropping my gaze.

Uncle Roy, Colin's father, gasped and choked on his cigar smoke, then turned his gaze on Colin. "You too, son?"

Colin nodded but didn't look up.

"Well, I guess the position could have been worse." Uncle Roy put his cigar in the ashtray.

My father sat silently for a few moments then slammed his fist onto the arm of his chair. "Luca. I can't believe you would go and do something so reckless."

"I don't know why you consider this reckless. You were never specific about why you didn't take the offer. I just assumed you didn't want to come back after being killed."

Colin looked at me through hooded eyes and gave a slight shrug. "Uncle Charles, is there a real reason you and Dad didn't want to be familiars?"

My dad jerked his head toward Colin. "Yes, boy. There is a reason. I told you two to follow in our footsteps. To not draw attention to yourselves and to lay low."

Colin raised his brows. "Yes, we remember that very clearly. But, Uncle Charles, that's not a reason. That, to me, is just advice, which we have taken."

Uncle Roy nudged my dad's arm. "You might as well tell them, Charles. There's no going back now."

My dad let out a heavy sigh and rubbed his temples. "It's because you are part celestial witch."

I cocked my brow. "Oh, well that explains absolutely nothing."

My dad stared at me, anger in his eyes. "Don't get smart, boy. I raised you better than that."

"Well, if you raised me so well, Dad, why didn't you give me a real reason to not take the offer if it arose? And don't tell me 'because

I told you so.' That's not a valid reason," I replied sarcastically, knowing I would get a reaction out of him.

My dad's jaw dropped, and he stared at me in shock, then he stood, raising his arm to backhand me.

"Charles Matthews. Don't you dare," my mom scolded from the screen door that led to the kitchen. "You tell your son your concerns, or I will. And don't leave anything out. This is your fault, you know. But honestly, I'm glad they took it."

My dad took a deep breath and sat back down. "Fine, I'll tell them."

My mom gave us a small smile and slipped back into the kitchen with Aunt Lilith. I glanced at Colin as he shifted in his seat.

My dad took a swig of his lemonade and leaned back. "Your grandfather was a full celestial witch, and your grandmother was half celestial and half green witch." He met my gaze.

"Yes. I'm aware," I replied.

He shook his head like the news was a hard pill to swallow. "Being a celestial witch carries a lot of responsibility and power."

I gave a quick nod.

"A celestial witch is far more powerful than a green witch, and that kind of power is addictive. Your grandfather spent years trying to harness more power. After I left home at sixteen, I got word from your grandmother that he had gone too far and discovered the side of evil, which gave him immense power. He was imprisoned for the next forty years before he killed himself." He leaned forward to rest his elbows on his knees and his head in his hands.

In all my life, I had never seen my dad so ashamed or embarrassed. I looked at Colin then Uncle Roy before turning back toward my dad. "I'm so sorry about that, Dad. I can understand your concern, but why didn't you just tell me? It's not like you followed in his footsteps."

"Your grandfather signed up at a young age. He was stripped of his familiar mark thirty-five years into his life sentence. They said stripping the mark from him weakened his powers and drove him mad. It was at that point that I promised your grandmother I would never accept the offer." He wiped his hands over his face and sat straighter. "That's why I never took it."

"I can understand that, but you aren't like him, and neither am I. I haven't even shown a sign of possessing celestial powers. I'm not sure I do." I sipped my lemonade and set the glass back down. "To be completely honest, even if I had known all of this, it wouldn't have changed my mind. I've always loved the thought of teaching other paranormal witches. The GWP can't force me to call upon my powers anyway."

My dad nodded. "Son, I really hope you're right. I can't stand the thought of this obsession passing to you." He stood and walked back inside, where he stayed for the evening.

The rest of our visit was normal. No one brought up the familiar conversation again. We helped our fathers bale the hay field and clean the animals' stalls. We even got to see one of the cows give birth. I told Colin he wasn't allowed to name her, though. Poor Mayo was tortured enough.

Chapter Four
Personal Journal Entries for Familiar Training

Colin

July 10, 1900

We start our training today. I still don't believe it will take us ten years to learn everything we need to know.

September 15, 1900

We've been going nonstop for the last two months. I may have been wrong about this taking us ten years to learn. We have been doing things with herbs that I didn't even know were possible. We leave in two days to visit the Paranormal Archives. I was unaware this place even existed. We will be studying there for the next six months.

September 25, 1900

We have arrived in London at the Paranormal Archives. I'm blown away by how big this place is. We have our own dorm rooms, and there's a field for training and a huge cafeteria. We don't need to leave the grounds unless we want to sightsee. On a side note, I'm not meant to be on the water at all. I was sick the entire ride. I'm not looking forward to the ride home on a freighter.

Luca

September 27, 1900

I could get used to the food here in London. Every morning, the in-house chef makes a large English breakfast for everyone. We have bacon, eggs, fried potatoes, grilled tomatoes, and even sausage. Not to mention the pastries, fruits, vegetables, meat and cheese trays, and tea, coffee, and lemonade they have available day and night. I'll need to walk five miles every day to keep combat ready. I could get used to eating like this.

October 12, 1900

Well, Colin and I have discovered that neither of us are made for the sea, whether it's riding its waves on a ship or eating the contents of its waters. They had something called *calamari* as a special for dinner today. We were excited to try it because of the fancy name, but little did we know, we are both allergic to squid. We were given something called *epinephrine*, which we were given through a syringe. The side effects were not the least bit fun.

November 15, 1900

Today, we were offered a once-in-a-lifetime experience that might knock at least one year off our studies. Professor Merlin—I know, the name is ironic, but at least he doesn't wear a robe—who teaches potions here at the Archives, is traveling around Europe and teaching different spells and potion classes. He offered for us to join him as his apprentices. We gladly accepted. We leave in March of next year.

December 29, 1900

We got our partners today for our trial run on familiar training. We won't bind to them, but they will report back to Professor Merlin about our progress at the end of January. My partner's name is Mika, and Colin is partnered with Mika's brother, Eli.

Colin

January 12, 1901

Having someone shadow us the past two weeks has been a little unnerving. Twenty more days, and they will report back to the professor about our teaching skills, patience, and knowledge. I wonder if we have a choice about who we bond to. It might be a little more comfortable to be at a female's beck and call.

February 2, 1901

We got our results back from our familiar pairing today. We passed aside from not being very personable. But the professor said that was normally the case when bound to the same gender. About ninety percent of pairings after graduation will be to the opposite gender so we won't feel tense standing so close to them while training—unless requested otherwise. It wasn't unheard of to have same-sex relationships.

Since passing all the classes with our partners, we were given the details of how our assignments will be. On average, our bindings will be two years, but the timing depends on the witch. We will be chosen by what we have to offer and our protection skills. More often than not, we will be chosen by the witches' parents or guardians since witches don't get their powers until they are eighteen. We have the right to decline any offers we are given and can choose to reverse the binding spell under dire situations, but the witch can choose to reverse it for any reason.

March 15, 1901

We are finished with our classes in London. We leave tomorrow with Professor Merlin on his trip through Europe. There will be twelve month-long stops with a week off between locations. This might be my last entry for a while due to our packed schedules. I will update once we get back to the States.

June 3, 1902

Over these past fifteen months, Luca and I have gained knowledge beyond our wildest dreams. Professor Merlin has given us an unforgettable experience under his apprenticeship. Luca and I have four journals of spells and potions, and I chose to take on extra lessons about charging stones and gems. I have a journal three-quarters full of charging spells I've written myself. As much as it pains us to end this experience with Professor Merlin, I look forward to being back in the States soon.

Luca

June 22, 1902

We arrived back home this morning. We will be visiting our parents for one month before going back to Salem to start our training assignments.

December 12, 1903

The past year and a half has been hectic. We have been on site learning how to hunt and capture werewolves, vampires, warlocks, lykens, and sirens, and we even helped a ghost cross over to the afterlife. I got word this morning that my father is ill and not expected to live much longer. Colin and I are taking a leave of absence to help my mom with this transition. She will move in with Aunt Lilith after his passing, and they will be combining the farms into one. Colin and I will be helping Uncle Roy build a new barn. Thankfully, we can continue some of our studies while on leave since they are just reading and reports on the different species in the world.

June 3, 1904

My father passed this morning, surrounded by me, my mom, Colin, Aunt Lilith, and Uncle Roy. His last month has been tough on my mom. My father didn't want to know anything about his illness aside from how long he might have. He survived a little over a month longer than the doctors expected. He got to see the new barn completed, and we moved him and my mom into Aunt Lilith's house last month. My father wanted to know that my mom would be looked after. He is finally at peace. We will be returning to our training at the end of the month.

August 1, 1909

We decided to forgo our entries unless something exciting came up. Well, it has. We have completed our familiar training with a year to spare and will be out on assignment for the GWP until we receive our first binding offer. That might be a few years.

Chapter Five

Report from Luca Matthews and Colin Jacobs

Binding to Luna and Lora Baker

December 1932–January 1935

This binding was offered by Luna and Lora Baker's father, Mr. Archer Baker. These two girls are identical twins and share the same interests outside of magic. They were presented to us as green witches with knowledge of this world since birth. Their father wanted them to learn the basic spells for healing, protection, and defense. They did not have any prior knowledge of these things before coming to us.

As of this binding's conclusion, the girls have full knowledge of making the healing and protection potions and charging stones, crystals, and gems for their healing and protection properties. Reversal of the binding spell was a mutual decision, and the bond was broken fully as of January 19, 1935.

Binding to Isla and Lola Goode

August 1945–October 1952

This binding was presented to us by Isla and Nola Goode's grandfather, Samual Goode. These two girls are cousins and have different interests outside of magic due to living so far apart since birth. They were presented as green witches with a possibility of weather manipulation. They were to be taught the basics of magic with concentration in stones, crystals, and gems. They have been aware of this world since turning sixteen years of age. Lola is seven months older than Isla. They do have some knowledge of what stones, crystals, and gems do, and they had knowledge of how to charge them for basic spells.

At the end of this binding, the girls have full knowledge of how to charge, clean, and deactivate stones for all purposes and are able to write a spell for a stone if needed in the future. They also have fair knowledge of herbal spells. As of this binding's conclusion, the girls have shown no interest in training for weather manipulation. Reversal of this binding spell was a mutual decision, and the bond has been fully severed as of October 22, 1952.

Binding to Ysma and Esme Blackwood

August 1960–January 1961

This binding was presented by the GWP. Ysma and Esma Blackwood were orphaned when their parents were killed in a raid. Their uncle raised them here in Salem from age five. The girls are almost one year apart, with Ysma being the youngest. The girls came of age two years ago and have since been arrested after doing spells in public. The GWP had hoped that they could be taught the ins and outs of their powers and what behaviors are unacceptable. They presented with green witch powers and knew quite a bit from their own research.

After we made multiple attempts to stop their use of powers in public, they were arrested again. They would not remain with us and often snuck out and locked us in the house after casting a sleeping spell on us. They are also being charged with assaulting a familiar and pursuing evil powers. To prevent them from harming others, Luca Matthews and I, Colin Jacobs, reversed the binding spell. This binding was not a mutual choice and was done as a safety precaution. The girls were presented back to the GWP for processing. They are not safe to be on their own. Possibility of going to the evil side.

Chapter Six
Personal Journal Entries

Luca

July 17, 1963

After our failed binding with Ysma and Esme, Colin and I decided to hold off on any more bindings. The stress of this last one was too much to bear.

June 2, 1969

We have been on an archaeological dig with members of the GWP in Canada for the past six months. I thought we would enjoy it, but it's like playing in a large sandbox that's been sifted clean of toys. They aren't exactly sure what we're searching for, but the seekers say it holds immense power.

April 4, 1976

We have yet to find anything of value or even power in the last eight years of digging. We are almost done with all nine sites where the power was located. We will be going back to the States in two months.

Colin

March 29, 1980

The Green Witch Project is getting ready to branch off and start the Greater World Protection company, which will be looking into ways to help more around the world and keep people safe whether they are paranormal or not. Luca and I will be aiding Tyson, head of IT, with stuff on the inside. After our bones heal, that is. Our last mission failed before it even started. I ended up with a broken leg and wrist, and Luca broke his collarbone and foot. We'll work inside the GWP for a while. There's a lot of work to be done. Atticus Jr. is really pushing for the Greater World Protection company to work. Private security is slowly starting to fade in people's day-to-day lives.

May 13, 1982

We were finally successful in making our first paranormal sensors for the security systems we hope to put up in everyone's houses. The Greater World Protection business will launch free systems in 1984 that will be able to detect fire and will have buttons to alert the police if they need assistance or an ambulance. The systems will also be able to track paranormal signals. They will all be run through the GWP, and any non-paranormal situations will be dispatched to local police. So far, this expansion will open more than one hundred locations worldwide and create thousands of new jobs.

December 23, 2000

We have been successfully fitting homes with the new systems that have cameras attached. Now, we can log into the cameras ourselves and view the footage before sending out either paranormal guards or the local police.

Luca

November 2, 2015

We have been working on the security systems side of the GWP for thirty-five years now. Colin and I are more than ready to get back out in the field. We're returning to missions and collecting rare artifacts that could potentially cause problems.

Chapter Seven

June 1, 2017

Luca

We got another assignment from Celeste Bane, daughter of Atticus Bane Jr. and the newly appointed leader of the GWP, who got promoted after working as second-in-command under her father for nine years. She was informed that some potions that had been kept with the Hazel Craig display were stolen from the museum. So, Colin and I were dispatched to find out more about what was in them and what the staff knew about the thief.

Upon arriving at the museum—the same one we stood outside in 1890 when the warlock dropped a potion grenade—they were closed, but an officer stood just inside the door and let us in, telling us where to go. Colin and I quickly took in the Hazel Craig display before heading to the hallway in the back of the large open room. The first door on the left was open, and I gently knocked on the door to avoid startling the lady inside.

"Hello, ma'am. My name is Luca Matthews, and this is Colin Jacobs. We're here to investigate the theft of some apothecary bottles that belonged to Hazel Craig."

She nodded and held out her hand to Colin and me. "Hello. My name is Carol Archer. I'm the museum coordinator. Please, follow me, and I'll take you to the display first."

We followed her back out into the open room and stopped just behind the display case. Carol bent to slide open the base of the display and pulled out a brochure that showed what the apothecary bottles looked like and what they supposedly held.

As I skimmed the information listed, I frowned. "Ma'am, could you please explain why something so dangerous would be out on display in the first place?"

Carol gestured toward a long hallway across the large room from her office. Colin and I followed her down it to a set of stairs that descended into a storage area. She sat behind a sizable desk to the right of the stair base. "Please, have a seat." She indicated the chairs on the other side of the desk. "The apothecary jars have never been opened to check on their contents, but without the spell to activate them, they were deemed safe."

My brows furrowed. "How are potions meant to steal someone's past, present, or future memories or lives deemed safe?" I asked, agitation building. "If these are supposedly from Hazel Craig's evil spell book, they should have been destroyed as soon as they were discovered. Not put on display."

Colin placed his hands on the edge of the desk and leaned toward Carol.

"We need to view the security footage from the past thirty days," he said, his voice low but firm. "How many camera angles are available?"

Carol cleared her throat and nodded. "Umm. Two cameras face the display."

Colin straightened. "I want the video feed for this entire location. Inside and out."

Carol turned the computer screen so Colin and I could view it. She glanced at me. "How would you like me to get you access? Email, flash drive, or would you like the security computer tower?"

"We will view the feed from the main monitoring screen here. That way we can make sure nothing was deleted or tampered with. And we will need a list of every single item that is displayed or in storage in this facility," Colin said.

"Yes, of course, gentlemen. I can give you full access to the security room and show you where to find the list of items." Carol rose and walked ahead quite briskly considering the height of her heels.

We had the advantage of keeping up due to her five-foot-two stature.

We spent the next two days in the security room watching all the video footage and getting face shots of potential thieves. We sent the images and feeds of the bottles being stolen back to Tyson, the IT guy who worked for the GWP.

After a quick chat with Celeste, we pulled the entire display due to Hazel Craig's dangerous background. We also pulled some other items that had been put on display from powerful paranormals. These items would be cloaked and hidden from view until someone more powerful could guard them.

We received a call from Tyson just as we were loading the last crate of artifacts into the truck. He managed to track the thief all the way through Salem using the security cameras spread throughout the town, down the highways, and into Shawsville. He gave us an address and the time the thief was last seen on camera, and we took the truck back to the GWP to get our car.

Colin and I had decided to put the top down on my '67 Camaro before we exited the GWP garage bay. As we got onto the highway headed toward Shawsville, Colin received a message from Tyson saying the thief was on the move. We arrived in Shawsville and parked a couple of blocks before the thief's last known location.

A few minutes later, Colin received another text with a photo of the car the man was driving. Tyson had tracked down the identity of the man through the local DMV and sent another photo of the man's driver's license and the tag number on his car in the photo.

After an hour of not getting an updated location from Tyson, we decided to drive the rest of the way to the man's last appearance. The vehicle was parked at the end of the driveway, and the man, Russell Carine—according to his license—was nowhere to be found. I grabbed my phone from the dashboard and called Tyson to give him an update. It seemed as if someone had come to pick the man up in another vehicle, or he fled on foot.

It would take Tyson a while to track down the man's location again, so Colin and I stopped for a quick dinner. Afterward, Tyson still hadn't located the man or any suspicious vehicles on the road.

For now, we were to wait in Shawsville until he could be found. Celeste dispatched a crew of seekers to see if they could track the man's location.

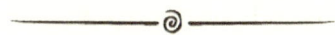

Just after midnight, we got a call from Tyson telling us to meet a man named Raymond Craig in Dropmore, a town just outside of Salem, Virginia.

I glanced at Colin as I pulled out from Russell's house, where we were keeping watch. "Okay, you look confused, dude. What's up?"

He shook his head and turned to me. "Isn't Raymond Craig a direct descendant of Hazel Craig, and doesn't he have the nightmare responsibility of keeping her spell book hidden?"

"Umm. Yeah, I think he is. I've never met him." I snuck another peek at Colin.

Colin glanced out the window as we pulled back onto the highway. "I wonder if he's evil like Hazel was said to be."

My eyebrow quirked at the comment. I had heard horrible stories of the death and destruction her spell book had left behind as it changed hands before Hector Craig found it almost one hundred years later. "Let's hope that's not the case."

We arrived in Dropmore thirty minutes later and stopped at the first motel we came to off the highway. Raymond was supposed to meet us there around one o'clock. Colin bought us some cold sodas from the vending machine, and I grabbed us a couple of bags of chips from our stash behind the seat of our car.

A little after one o'clock, a voice startled me out of my daze.

"Matthews and Jacobs, I presume." A white-haired man approached us from the side of the street opposite to where I was watching the leaves of a Japanese maple tree blow in the wind.

I opened the car door and climbed out, holding my hand out to the man in front of me. "Hello, sir. You must be Mr. Craig."

He gave a nod. "Yes, I am. But please, call me Raymond."

Colin walked around the car and shook Raymond's hand. "It's nice to meet you, sir. Are you the one they called in to locate Russell?"

"Yes. I'm afraid I have some good news and some bad news. I have located him, but he's surrounded by eight other men quite a bit larger than the likes of us." Raymond rubbed the edge of his thinning hairline.

Colin tilted his head. "Did you notice if any used magic?"

"Thankfully, no. I can't sense that they have any either. This may be a case of mere mortals going after power," he said.

"No worries, then, sir. Can you do encasing wards?" I felt around in my pocket for my black onyx ring. Normally, we just had to keep it close to cast simple spells, but since we would be going up against at least nine men, it was best to have it on my finger.

Raymond rubbed his chin. "Yes, I can do them. Are you thinking of encasing them one at a time or all together?"

I considered the question. "We should probably encase them in groups of two or three so we can process them and bind them before questioning."

"That sounds like a perfect plan, young man. I like the way you think."

"Thank you, sir. Could you possibly show us the way?" I gestured toward where Raymond had approached us from.

"We'll need to drive. He's about six blocks down. I posted a guard to ensure we don't lose him again." Raymond jerked his chin toward my car. "Do you mind if I ride along? I've never been in a car like this before."

I gave him a quick smile, and we all climbed into the Camaro. We drove to the location and parked around the corner. It appeared as if they were in an old, abandoned hardware store with plywood covering the building's front windows. Light seeped out from inside.

We walked across the street from the abandoned shop and stood in the shadows as we waited for backup and the transport bus.

A man in all black stepped outside. We could hear him arguing with someone on the phone but couldn't quite make out what he said. He lit the cigarette hanging from his mouth and took a big puff, then slowly let it out before continuing the argument.

My phone vibrated in my pocket, and I ducked behind a tree to check the message so the guy wouldn't see the light from my screen. It was our backup saying they had arrived and were surrounding the back exits. As I walked out from behind the tree, the man yelled "Whatever!" into the phone then hung up and went back inside.

I leaned closer to Colin and Raymond. "Backup is surrounding all the other entrances. Are you ready?"

Raymond flashed a quick smile. "I was born ready, son. Binding three groups of three men should be just fine. I'll blast the door down. You two storm in and encase the first six. I'll grab the rest."

We exchanged a nod and started across the street. The guard who had been watching from his car a couple of buildings down saw us approaching the building and made his way up to us.

Raymond turned to the guard. "Grab anyone we miss, would ya, Marvin?"

Marvin took a step back and reached into his pocket to slip on his black onyx ring. Colin and I stood on either side of the door to allow Raymond room to safely blast the door down without hitting us with debris.

A split second later, Colin and I rushed the main room with our right hands out, ready to perform the encasing spell. We surveyed the room, and the men were spread out around two tables. They all jumped up when we entered, drawing guns, knives, and even a baseball bat. I went for four men that were closest together as they tried to come at us from the other side of the table.

As if it were planned, Colin and I chanted "*Condescendere aliquem*" in unison.

Our magic swirled through the air like an invisible lasso, surrounding four men in my encasement and four in Colin's, all while disarming them.

A man fitting Russell's description ran toward the back of the building as Raymond entered through the door he had just blasted off its hinges. A few moments later, the man stepped backward into the front room once more, his hands up in surrender. One of the men from our backup team had his fist pointed at Russell as he entered the room.

Raymond glanced around. "Well, that was easier than I expected." He turned his full attention to Russell. "I'll take that bag on your back, young man. It does not belong to you."

Our backup from outside all filed in and kept an eye on the men we had encased. I approached Russell and took the bag from him then handed it to Raymond. "Keep a close eye on these men and give them a nonlethal blast if they move. I'll search and disarm them of anything dangerous."

Raymond stood back a bit and let Colin and me pat down each man, starting with Russell. By the time we were done with them, they were free of weapons and personal possessions—their money, wallets, jewelry, and phones were bagged and tagged and ready for Sheriff Timothy Veron of the Salem Police Department to take them away. Though they had stolen magic-imbued items, not one of the nine men had a black onyx ring or any possessions that showed they were paranormal. So this would be a matter for the normal police.

Veron had just recently been sworn in as the sheriff in Salem after moving his way up the chain. He had paranormal powers, as did a few deputies, but they were the only ones who knew of the paranormal happenings around the world.

The nine men were all confused by our methods of taking them down, but once they were processed at the department, their memories of the capture would be erased, and another scenario would be put in its place.

It took a couple of hours to get them all processed at the station. While Veron started on the paperwork, Colin and I stood outside with Raymond.

"I have to admit, I was very impressed with you during the capture and the care you took making sure the men were completely unarmed." Raymond crossed his arms over his chest and leaned against the building.

Colin raised his brows. "Yes, we learned the hard way on that one after a warlock in our custody pulled out a potion grenade and killed five of us on the spot. We've been very thorough about disarming criminals since then."

Raymond tilted his head and raised his brows. "That would do it. Are you two currently bound to anyone or training?"

I dropped my gaze to my hands and shook my head. "We haven't done a binding since 1961. I guess you could say it didn't go well. We ended up learning a lesson on that one as well."

Raymond sighed. "That's a shame. It would be hard to have a binding turning bad. Then again, I married my familiar. Unfortunately, I lost her in 2002 to someone trying to get their hands on Hazel's spell book."

I glanced at Raymond. "I'm so sorry to hear that, Raymond. I couldn't imagine how difficult that must have been."

He softly shook his head. "My granddaughters are thirteen years old, and I have been searching for the perfect familiars for them. I know you said you had a bad experience with your last binding, but will you please just consider trying again? I think you two would be perfect for my Rosebud and Daisy."

"Do they know anything about this life?" I asked.

He shook his head. "Not that I am aware of. Rosebud is into a lot of the spookier stuff like movies and books, and Daisy is more of the laid-back one. They both know the term *green witch*, but they aren't aware of the powers that go along with it. They just think it works like a witch doctor who works with voodoo. Rosebud is into herbals, and Daisy is into stones, crystals, and gems. I have instilled knowledge in them that will help them along their path, but it will be up to them to find it." He lowered his arms and tucked his thumbs into his pockets. "Their parents don't have paranormal powers, so it was up to me to make their transition into this life safe. Maybe if they have to work for it, they will appreciate it more and stay on the side of good."

I glanced at Colin. "*What do you think?*" I asked him telepathically.

"*Raymond is definitely not what I expected from a descendant of Hazel Craig, but we can talk it over tonight and let him know tomorrow.*" Colin turned to Raymond. "It sounds like these girls will need a lot of guidance. Luca and I will discuss it tonight. Where will you be tomorrow? We will come and let you know either way."

Raymond perked up at the possibility of us saying *yes*. "Thank you for considering it. I will be at my shop all day tomorrow, Roots & Remedies. It's located on Main Street here in town."

Colin gave him a curt nod. "We'll stop by tomorrow around noon."

Raymond extended his hand to us. Colin and I both shook it.

Then Raymond placed his hand on my shoulder to steady himself for a moment. "I look forward to it, boys. Either way. This has been an impressive assignment." Without another word, he went inside the police station.

Colin and I turned to head back to the Camaro. We had a lot to think about. If the girls were anything like Raymond, binding with them could be successful. But our binding with Ysma and Esme had proven dangerous and impossible. Maybe this would be the change we needed in our lives as familiars The girls were still young, so we would still have time to learn more about Rosebud and Daisy before they came of age and got their powers.

Chapter Eight

June 6, 2017

Colin

Luca and I stopped at Ms. Lucy's Pancake House and asked if Raymond had a favorite meal. We placed our order and arrived at Roots & Remedies a few minutes before noon.

Raymond was helping a customer, but he smiled and gestured for us to go back into the back room to wait for him. As we stepped behind the curtain, we expected it to be a storeroom with a worktable for the mortar and pestle, but instead, we stood in a fully functional kitchen, dining table and all.

After a few minutes, the customer left, and Raymond closed the shop for lunch.

"Hello, gentlemen. You didn't need to bring me lunch." He glanced at the third Styrofoam tray on the table. "What's the occasion?"

I let out a little huff and smiled. "No occasion exactly. We knew you were at work and that our conversation might take time, so we thought we could eat and chat. Everybody's gotta eat." I looked to Luca for backup.

"Well, I appreciate it. I wasn't sure what I would eat for lunch anyway." Raymond sat at the table, unfolded a napkin, and placed it on his lap. "Have you gentlemen heard anything from Veron about Russell and his crew?"

Luca shook his head as he took a bite of his burger. "No, nothing yet. Is there already news to report?" he asked with a stuffed cheek.

Raymond shook his head as he cut into his Salisbury steak and onions. "Not that I know of. I just hope the processing goes smoothly. I'm not sure what will happen to the other eight men, because they weren't directly involved in the theft, but I'm sure they will get charged for aiding and abetting. As they should."

Luca and I nodded in agreement but didn't say anything else on the matter. A few moments and a bite or two later, I cleared my throat and moved my gaze to Raymond. "So, we've been thinking about the offer you made yesterday. I know we have about five years before we would take them on for training, but could you tell us more about your granddaughters? We are willing to take a chance on them."

A smile spread across Raymond's face as he wiped his mouth with his napkin. "Well, as you probably know, Rosebud and Daisy aren't their real names. Rosebud is actually Sadie, and Daisy is Isadora. We call her Izzy for short. They are a little less than a month apart in age. Isadora is unaware that she is my granddaughter. I have always treated her as my own, but after what happened with my son and daughter when they were younger, I thought it would be best to let them think they were best friends from birth. Maybe harm wouldn't come to them if they knew nothing about the truth of our family or the magical world." He sighed heavily. "I may come to regret keeping their true relationship a secret, but I can't change that now. They aren't ready."

"How do you think they will take it?" Luca asked.

"I'm not sure, but I have always treated them equally. Izzy even calls me Pops. I do plan on telling them when they graduate high school and move here to help me with my shop, which has always been their dream." He smiled.

I took a drink of my lemonade. "Have they started showing signs of their powers?"

Raymond nodded. "They have as of their last birthday. At Sadie's thirteenth birthday party, something made her really focus on her birthday-candle flames. Out of the blue, she reached up and tried to touch the flame, and it sort of grew around her fingers before going out when she pinched the wick." Raymond ate a bite of his mashed potatoes. "A couple of weeks after Izzy turned thirteen, she was trying to get down off her top bunk and fell. She screamed, and when my daughter, Sylvia—Izzy's mother—went to check on her, she said she felt like she was floating for a few moments before she made contact with the floor." He checked the calendar on the wall beside the fridge then took another bite of his potatoes. "I think it's been a couple of weeks now, but my son, Elliott—Sadie's father—called saying that Sadie told him a stray cat had asked her for a can of Fancy Feast. They've never owned a cat, so Elliott said it was strange that she would know a brand of cat food."

My quirked brows lowered. "Those are some pretty strange powers to manifest at this age. I can see the talking cat being her spirit power, but what are you thinking the other two signs indicate?" I took another bite of my burger.

"If I had to guess, I would say elemental powers, fire and air. I am unaware of my ancestors over the last hundred years possessing elemental powers aside from spirit, but I would assume it's possible."

I frowned at Luca. "Those seem like some pretty strong powers at their age, but it's not unheard of. We would love the chance to train them as their familiars. I know they have a few more years before they will be ready, but we will check in every six to nine months for an update on their progress. Oh... umm. They weren't raised in Salem, right? I guess that should have been our first question."

Raymond chuckled. "Oh my, no. Their parents have lived in Richmond since before they were conceived. I assume your last binding paranormals were raised here."

Luca's eyes went wide. "Yes. As much promise as they showed at the beginning, evil pulled them in faster than I thought possible."

Concern filled Raymond's eyes. "That is the one downfall for a child growing up in Salem. The chance for evil to take over is much too high."

We finished our lunch, and with the promise to check in as often as possible, we left Roots & Remedies with a new appreciation for the Craig bloodline. Since 1872, the only thing that had ever been said about the Craig bloodline was bad. Though Hazel Craig had been killed in the witch trials two hundred years before, her evil deeds had never been forgotten. Luca and I wanted to help change that perspective if possible.

As promised, Luca and I checked in with Raymond as often as possible. We would bring him lunch, and he would fill us in on Sadie and Izzy and their possible powers. Currently, Raymond believed they could have all five of the elemental powers between them. To have all five of the elemental powers when their parents had no paranormal powers at all was very rare in itself. Sadie and Izzy could prove to be exactly what we needed against the forces of evil.

Chapter Nine

October 17, 2021

Luca

We stopped by Roots & Remedies to see if Raymond had any updates for us about the girls. He was closing up the shop for the day and invited us back to his house for dinner. Raymond had prepped a tray of his homemade lasagna the night before and said he would love for us to join him.

After dinner, during which Colin and I ate way too much of the lasagna and garlic bread, we went into the living room to chat some more. While listening to Raymond's story about what the girls planned to do after graduation, a wave of intense sensation rolled through my body. I glanced at Colin with wide eyes.

"I swear, the timing is always off with these demons." Raymond paused to study Colin and me as we swayed. "You boys okay?" Concern etched his face.

I nodded. "We're being pulled into the..." I squinted as the sensation crawled into my head. "Underworld," I finished as I glanced around our surroundings.

We stood inside a prison cell. The bars were rusty, and the floor was made of stone and very dirty.

Colin took a deep breath before releasing it. "They call upon us for help, but we always end up in some sort of prison hold. You would think these demons would approach us with wine and a feast before asking for assistance."

"That will never happen in our realm, mortal," someone said from behind us.

We slowly turned to face three men standing just outside the cell.

"What do you demons want now? We were in the middle of something." Colin approached the bars.

A quick blast of sparks shot from one of the men's open hands and hit Colin square in the chest, slamming him into the stone wall at the back of the cell.

The man in the middle turned to me. "Anything smart to say, mortal?"

"Smart, no. But I will repeat his question. What do you want from us?" I stared the demon down.

His eyes shifted from a dark gray to solid black as an evil smile formed on his face. He gave the man to his left a nod, and the man pulled a set of old keys from his pocket and came to unlock the cell. He grabbed my arm and dragged me out before binding my hands behind me. The man that had blasted Colin went in and pulled him out of the cell and into the next room. The man holding me pushed me in the same direction.

By the time my eyes adjusted to the lack of light in the window-less cell, I watched the man dragging Colin slam him down into a wooden chair and bind his hands behind him. I was forced into the chair facing Colin. The man released my right hand and wrapped the bindings around the back of the chair before retying my wrist.

I studied Colin for a few moments—to make sure he was still breathing—before I searched for the man who seemed to be in charge. He gave a loud grunt, and the other two men scurried from the room, closing the wooden door behind them.

The room looked to be a mixture of a study and interrogation chamber. A stand on the far side of the room held a large book that I assumed was the demons' version of a spell book. The room's condition made it feel like we'd been transported back to a time before electricity was invented. The candles lit all around the room dripped wax from their holders. The floors were made of rough-cut wood, as were the tables and chairs spread across the large space.

The man pulled up a chair to the right of me and sat to stare at Colin. "Your friend here will be punished if you don't agree to my requests."

I watched the demon with disgust. "Why don't you torture me instead? It looks like your guy already did enough damage."

A wicked smile formed across his face, and his gray eyes darkened to almost black. "That can be arranged, mortal."

I released the breath I'd been holding. "What's your request?" I asked, trying to keep the anger out of my voice.

"A man in your realm has something I want. I want you to get rid of him and bring the item to me." He lifted his arms above his head and laced his fingers behind it, then leaned back.

My brows furrowed. "Okay. Let me see if I have this correct. You want me to kill someone and bring you something they have?"

The demon nodded.

"Are you aware of what tasks you can call upon us for? Because this is not one of them. We can help you with spells or bring you herbs or send a message to someone in our realm, but we cannot be called upon to kill for you."

His eyes went completely black, and he reached into his pocket and pulled out a rolled cigarette. He stomped his boot on the floor twice, and the man who'd bound me to the chair came back into the room.

The head demon nodded toward me. "Tie his hands to the arms of his chair and make sure he can't get out."

The man did as he was told, undoing my bindings. He pulled my arms forward so my fingers wrapped around the edges of the armrests and rebound my hands one at a time. Without a word or a glance in his boss's direction, he walked back out the door.

The demon's eyes had turned back to gray as if the cigarette was calming him. He scooted his chair closer to mine then leaned in. "Are you sure that is the answer you want to give me, mortal?"

"No. But it's the only answer I can give you. We would be stripped of our powers and killed if we harmed someone in our realm at your request."

He nodded and blew smoke at me, and I closed my eyes. A sharp pain shot through my hand below the bottom joint of my thumb, and my eyes flew open. He had put the cigarette out on my skin and was holding it there. I clenched my teeth to keep from crying out in pain.

After the smoke had dissipated, his eyes moved up to mine, and they were black again. "It's funny that you think I'm giving you an option. I'm not asking you to do this. You will agree to it. If you don't, I will end you myself. And I am not a patient man."

I tried moving my hand to give the tight skin relief beneath the burn, but with the position of my restraints, it only provided a small respite. "Then I guess you will have to kill me. Because I won't harm my people."

The demon clenched his fists as he stood, and I held my breath, waiting for his punch to make contact. The first one hit me square in the ribs, knocking the breath out of me. The next one found the right side of my face.

As I tried to catch my breath, he turned his attention to Colin, kicking his foot. "Once this one wakes up, you might be more agreeable."

Without another word, he left.

As much as I wanted Colin to be okay, I hoped he stayed out for a while. Thankfully, the rules for pulling a familiar into another realm stated that they couldn't keep us for more than two hours. They could only give us the request then release us.

The GWP had sensors all over the world that could track when a familiar was pulled into the underworld. If the time went longer than the two hours, the demon in charge of calling familiars to their bodies after they die would be contacted. Rumor had it, this demon who could drag any familiar from the underworld wasn't one to go up against. She was more of a kill-first-because-the-questions-don't-matter kind of demon, someone I hoped to never cross paths with.

Thankfully, I could still see my watch, even though I was bound. When I twisted my wrist a bit to see what time it was, I noticed the binding was looser than I'd thought. I tried my other hand, and it was a bit tighter, but if I moved enough, I could possibly get loose.

I worked at the restraints and finally got my left hand free. My right hand could easily slip loose if I needed. Colin was still out cold, so I knew I just had to be patient. I wrapped my binding around the arm of the chair but tucked the end under my wrist so the demon wouldn't see I was unbound when he came back in.

About an hour later, I could have sworn I heard someone say my name, but it was very distant, so I couldn't be sure.

A moment later, the demon came back into the room and sat in his chair. "So, are you ready to agree to my terms now?"

I stared at the demon as if I was considering his offer. I heard my name again then heard the same voice call Colin. "Can you tell me who it is that has this item you want?"

The demon smiled and pulled out another cigarette. "It doesn't work that way. You know this person, and if I told you, you would never agree."

The voice calling my name seemed to only be audible to me. The demon showed no signs of hearing anything. I concentrated on a piece of split wood in the floor as I tried to understand what the voice was saying. After another few moments, I could clearly hear Raymond chanting a spell from outside the demon realm. He was going to get us out.

I tried to get a better look at the room, to see if I could grab anything to take back with us so we could learn more about this realm and the black-eyed demon. The large book still lay on the table across the room, and I knew I needed to grab it. I listened to Raymond as he neared the end of his chant. He had told us that he wanted the girls to learn his technique of chanting certain retrieval spells and such. I could only hope he was using that same ending.

The demon was watching me, and I lifted my chin to meet his eye.

"What do I get out of this deal if I agree?" I asked.

The demon responded just like I had hoped. Raymond was saying the last part that he said he added to all of his spells, and as he said, "By my will," I jumped up and punched the demon square in the nose, knocking him back. Then I darted across the room, grabbing the large spell book just as Raymond said, "will it be."

A tingling sensation shot through my body, faster this time, as I was pulled back into our realm. I tried to regain my balance before I opened my eyes. After a few moments, Colin slowly came into focus. He sat in the same chair he'd been bound to, but we were in Raymond's living room. I turned to find Raymond standing at the edge of the couch.

He took a step closer to me and indicated my hand then my cheek. "We should get you cleaned up, Luca."

Without another word, Raymond went into the dining room and opened his apothecary cabinet to pull out a jar of salve. He gently took my hand and put a gob of it on the burn the demon had given me. He headed into the kitchen, and I followed. He grabbed a bag from the drawer and filled it with ice, then wrapped it in a towel. He brought it to me and put it against my cheek, then raised my hand to hold it in place.

I gave him a grateful nod, and he smiled then turned back to the living room to release Colin from his bindings. I helped Raymond lay Colin on the couch. Then Raymond sat on the love seat before looking up at me.

"What did the demon want with you?" Concern filled his eyes.

I spent a few minutes telling him what had happened and what the demon wanted. Raymond assured me that we would never be pulled back to that realm again.

Chapter Ten

October 18, 2021

Colin

Luca and I met Raymond at Roots & Remedies for lunch, as per his request. I had finally woken up at around eight o'clock last night with a pounding headache. Mason had given me a quick once over when we got back to the GWP, and I was cleared for fieldwork.

Raymond gestured for us to make ourselves comfortable in the kitchen while he finished up with his customer. After he locked up for lunch, he joined us, pulling the curtain closed across the doorway.

He must have seen my expression. "What? I don't want anyone to see you change into your familiar forms. People are always looking through the front windows when I close for lunch."

My brows rose briefly. "Oh, I didn't realize that we would be changing forms."

He gave a quick nod. "I've written a spell that will hide you from the demon world as if you were in a current binding. I don't think you've seen the last of that demon. He is evil beyond all meaning of the word."

Luca and I nodded in agreement. Luca rubbed the burn mark on his hand from the demon's cigarette and winced at the reminder. The bruise the demon had left under his eye was starting to feel better after using the arnica ointment Raymond had given him before we left his house last night. I didn't know what he put in his remedies, but I wouldn't go without them again if I could help it. Luca said they'd worked almost immediately.

Raymond worked on an herbal concoction for a few minutes. "With the normal binding spell, it's just the incantation itself, as you already know, but I need you to drink this so you have something for the binding to attach to since there isn't a physical person." He opened the door that went out to the greenhouse behind his shop and came back a moment later, carrying a large mirror.

I grabbed two teacups from the cabinet and set them beside Raymond's mortar and pestle. I filled the teapot sitting on the stove and turned on the burner to heat the water. Raymond split the contents of the mortar evenly into the teacups, and once the water was hot, I poured it over the herbs.

After drinking the tea, Luca and I changed into our cat forms and stood side by side in front of the mirror leaning against the cabinet. Raymond chanted the incantation, and I could feel a connection to the herbs in the tea just like I could when we bound to a physical being.

Raymond nodded. "You may feel a little lightheaded after you change back, so just brace yourselves, boys."

We changed back into our human forms, and the lightheaded feeling was quite a bit stronger than I thought it would be. I stayed still and closed my eyes as I waited for my equilibrium to level out.

When I opened my eyes again, I found Raymond's gaze. "Wow, this is a totally different feeling than binding with a person. Will this lightheadedness go away?"

Raymond chucked. "Yes, you will be fine in about an hour. It's more of a buzz from the tea than anything."

"Oh good," Luca said. "We're supposed to meet with Celeste at five so she can extract our memories, and I need to give her this book." He gestured toward his bag hanging on the back of his chair. "I can't read a word of it. I hope Tyson can translate it."

Raymond laughed again. "If Tyson can't decipher it, I know he will call in anyone he thinks might."

We chuckled at that. Tyson was always determined to find out details about what came into the GWP. If it was something he couldn't figure out, he would summon whoever might be able to "crack the code" as Tyson always said.

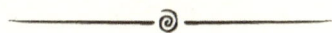

I handed the book to Celeste, and she carefully opened it. She flipped through a few pages and let out a little huff. "Boy oh boy is

Tyson going to have fun with this one," she said in her heavy Scottish accent. Though she was born and raised in Virginia, her family origins were from Scotland. As a child, she would talk in a pretend Scottish accent, and over the years, she had perfected it. Now, if she tried to talk without it, she couldn't do it without laughing. It was something her father, Atticus Jr., would joke about with her.

Celeste pushed a button on her phone, and Tyson came in on the other end. "Hey, Ty, I have a puzzle for you. You wanna come grab it now, or would you like me to put it in with the rest?"

"Oh, no, ma'am. I'll come get it right now." Excitement filled his voice.

She closed her eyes and giggled. "Boys and their toys. I will never understand." She glanced toward me and Luca and folded her hands in front of her.

Tyson came bustling into her office, and Celeste pointed to the book sitting on her desk.

He gently picked it up. "Origin?"

She gave him a small smile. "The underworld," she replied in an almost sultry voice. She waited for the words to roll around in Tyson's brain for a moment.

He looked up with his famous evil grin. "Oh, this one is gonna be fun." He quickly disappeared from the room.

Celeste giggled again and gestured toward the chairs. "Okay, boys, let me see these memories." She moved her fingers toward our temples.

The process of extracting our memories was painless, but it left a tingling sensation for a few seconds.

She took a step back and placed the smokelike strands into a jar and sealed them. "I'll log these tonight. How are you boys doing? Raymond said he was torturing you."

I nodded. "I was knocked out cold by one of his men and unconscious the entire time. Luca was the unfortunate one."

Luca turned his cheek into the light so she could see the massive bruise. She walked over to him and gently ran her fingers over the discoloration. Luca flinched.

"My apologies, Luca. I just wanted to make sure the bone wasn't broken underneath. Raymond said the demon also burned you."

Luca held out his hand.

She lifted it and studied the cigarette burn so she could log it with his memories. "This one was probably worse than the blow to the face." She hovered over the wound with her thumb for a moment, careful not to make contact. "You will have a pretty nasty scar, but there's no nerve damage. Thankfully."

Celeste had many amazing powers. She could extract memories, and once they were logged, she could read a report and see the memories as clear as day. She could also sense damage to anything within a two-inch surface. She couldn't fix the damage, but she could feel it. She was always going over people's superficial injuries, even after they'd been checked by Mason. The doctor would never live it down if he missed a fracture or infection and Celeste discovered it. In another life, she might have gone to medical school, though she denied it anytime Mason suggested it.

Chapter Eleven

May 3, 2022

Luca

I received a call from Raymond today. Sadie and Isadora would be starting college next week. He wanted us to go to Richmond to keep an eye on them, just in case they stumbled across their powers since they were almost of age. Sadie would be eighteen October 9, and Isadora would turn eighteen November 3.

Colin and I arrived in Richmond with a notebook of all the girls' information, including a copy of their graduation pictures so we could identify them. Thankfully, we opted to bring the van.

We made a deal with the paranormal couple that owned the corner store. They let us park the van in the back parking lot every night as long as we kept an eye on the store too. The girls still resided with their parents, next door to each other, a few houses down from the corner store. The shop owners agreed to keep up our cover story about us being hired security for as long as possible.

A few stores around Richmond had recently been broken into in the middle of the night, so the alibi worked.

We planned to follow the girls from their houses each morning to the college. Raymond wanted us to change up the van's glamours every few days so the girls wouldn't think they were being stalked. Although, it felt like that was exactly what we were doing.

The girls had their college orientation today, so we did a quick search of the area around their house to look for anything suspicious we should keep an eye on.

We tried to keep our human forms hidden from the students since rumors traveled quickly around the school. So, to all the college students, Colin and I would be the feral cats that lived on campus.

Two weeks into watching the girls, Sadie met a guy named Nate, and they seemed to hit it off pretty well. A couple of weeks later, Isadora met his twin brother, Ryan. Raymond didn't want us to interfere with their lives during college, so we stayed back, lounging around campus, hissing at anyone who tried to pet us.

The one thing that Raymond always told us since we had met him was that he wanted the girls to learn their life lessons, such as dating the wrong person, the effects of not putting oil in their cars, and so on. But when rumors started two months after the girls met Nate and Ryan, we knew we might need to intervene for their safety.

Two months after meeting the boys, Sadie and Izzy broke things off with them. Shortly after, a few college students said that they saw Nate and Ryan stalking Sadie and Isadora. That was all we needed to hear.

Once the girls made it home safe after class, Colin and I went to find Nate and Ryan in our human forms. We found them at the local bar. They were almost too drunk to stand, so we followed them back to their dorm in our feline forms to wait for them to sober up before confronting them.

At around two in the morning, we could tell that they had sobered up some, and Smokey scratched at the door to get them to open it. Once they did, we darted inside and jumped up on the table. As Nate closed the door behind him, he turned to me and Smokey, fussing at us for being on the table. Ryan swung at me, and Smokey shot a quick knockout spell at him then Nate.

The spell allowed us time to change back to our human forms and bind them to chairs. A few minutes later, they came to. They were disoriented due to the alcohol lingering in their systems, so it took them a moment longer than normal to figure out where they were.

Nate stared at me for a moment. "Who in the hell are you? And where the hell did those cats go?"

Colin shrugged and stretched a rubber band he found on the floor. "The cats aren't the ones you need to worry about now."

Ryan quirked his brow at me and Colin. "Oh yeah, and who is it that we need to be worried about, then? It's definitely not gonna be you," he slurred, trying to get up from his chair but realizing he was tied to it.

I rolled my eyes and stood from my chair. "Rumor has it that you meatheads are stalking two young ladies who broke up with you last week."

Nate tried to get free from his bindings but failed. "Yeah, so what if we are? What business is it of yours? Are you the hoes' new boyfriends?"

My eyes widened at that comment, and I glanced at Colin. Rage filled his gaze, and he balled his fists.

I put my hand out toward Colin to keep him back. "No. You can just think of us as the guys who warned you to leave them alone. Is that going to be a problem?" I asked, trying to keep my tone even.

Nate huffed. "Yeah, I'll stalk anyone I wanna stalk," he slurred.

Colin started toward Nate and Ryan, pulling their chairs closer to each other, then he leaned into their faces. "That's the wrong answer. Are you going to change it, or do you need to be convinced?"

Nate rolled his shoulders. "You need to change it. Nobody tells us what to do."

Colin took a step back and formed a ball of energy with his hand. Nate and Ryan seemed to sober up almost immediately as Colin studied them.

"What's wrong? You look like you've seen a ghost," he teased, an evil grin forming on his face.

Ryan squirmed in his seat. "What the hell are you two?"

"Like I said a minute ago, we're the warning," I said, stepping up beside Colin.

"We'll report you. You can't harass us like this. It's illegal." Nate glanced at Ryan.

Colin laughed. "Oh, I wanna see how that goes. I can picture it now. You go in and tell the dean that two cats came into your dorm and changed into humans to threaten you."

Nate's and Ryan's eyes went wide.

"The dean would just think you're high on something and expel you. But to you, the real issue will come when your mommy and daddy find out that you got expelled due to drugs. Then what do you think they'll do?"

I chuckled. "Oh, to be a fly on the wall during that conversation. If rumors are true, you two are trust-fund babies and won't get the billion-dollar inheritance from your grandparents unless you graduate with honors."

Nate's and Ryan's faces were priceless. Nate tried speaking but tripped over his words.

I held up a finger to quiet him and looked at Colin. "I think they are going to leave Sadie and Isadora alone from now on. They probably won't talk to them at all, even if the girls initiate a conversation. They're just going to walk away with their tails tucked between their legs." Ryan puffed out his chest. "We don't have tails."

Nate tried to elbow him, but his bindings held fast. "Shut up, you moron." He turned toward us. "You have our word that we will leave the girls alone and avoid contact at all costs."

I glanced at Colin. "Do you believe them? I don't know if I do."

Nate started stammering again. "I, um, I mean we will leave Sadie and Isadora alone as well as all the other girls on this campus. And we won't tell anyone about you two either. As far as I'm concerned, this was a dream."

"Good. One thing to remember is that we will be watching to make sure you don't slip up. Anytime you see a cat or even a dog on this campus, remember this encounter and be on your best behavior. There are many more out there like us, and we all protect the ones who can't protect themselves." Colin gave them a stare that would be etched into their minds.

We turned to leave the dorm room, and Ryan tried sitting up further in his chair. "You can't just keep us tied up. Someone will believe us if you leave us like this."

I turned to Nate and raised my hand. Snapping my fingers, I released his bindings.

Nate stood with a curt nod. "Thank you, and you have my word."

Ryan huffed. "But they don't have mine."

Nate jerked his head toward his twin brother and punched him square in the nose. He turned to us as Ryan moaned in pain. "You have his word too. Ryan just doesn't know it yet."

I jerked my chin in acknowledgment and snapped my fingers again, releasing Ryan's bindings. His hand went directly to his nose as he rolled out of the chair and onto the floor.

Colin opened the door, and we took one step out into the hall.

"We'll see you around campus, boys. Enjoy the rest of your evening," Colin said sarcastically as he pulled the door shut behind us.

We saw Nate and Ryan around campus every now and then, but if they spotted us in cat form, they tucked their heads and went the other way. They even shied away from the pigeons that sat outside the cafeteria, waiting for students to drop scraps for them.

We considered the intervention a success. We even heard rumors that Ryan claimed he had fallen and broken his nose. I couldn't say what Nate had told him, but it seemed to give Ryan a new perspective. They hadn't even been seen at the local bar after that.

Chapter Twelve

May 15, 2023

Colin

I couldn't wait to go back to Salem next week. Staying around this campus for the last year was torture. The drama that came with it was stressful.

Sadie and Isadora would be spending the summer with Raymond in Salem. Once they arrived, Raymond intended to tell them about the paranormal witch world. I wasn't sure how they would take the news, but I couldn't imagine it would be easy. He was supposed to let us know how the talk went and when he was ready for us to meet them.

A few weeks ago, the girls tried approaching us in our cat forms when we were on the steps of the college trying to stay out of the rain. I thought I might have to blast Luca. Sadie was about a foot away before he started backing up so she couldn't touch him. After the girls left, I asked Luca what he was thinking. He said he'd been mesmerized by her and kinda went numb for a moment.

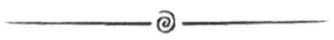

We left Salem a couple of hours after we saw Sadie packing her car. For some reason, it looked as if she would be driving by herself. I hadn't heard anything from Raymond, so I assumed he didn't know.

Raymond had asked us to give him one week to make contact before stopping by the shop. He wanted to give the girls time to adjust to the news before bringing us in.

Since we had time, we decided to check in at the GWP then visit Shawsville for a couple of days. Although our parents had passed, the farm was still ours. A farmhand lived in the house and took care of the animals and kept up with repairs.

Mayo-Neighs and Grimsley were buried at the back of the pasture along with some of the others we had lost over the years, including some family dogs and cats my mom had rescued against my dad's wishes.

After stopping by and visiting my uncle's great-granddaughter, Savannah—our last living relative—we headed to the house to check in. Luca fixed us Raymond's famous lasagna and garlic bread, and we called it a night. We woke early the next morning to give Frank a much-needed break, though we had to insist he take it. He still woke early, but he went to spend the morning with his daughter.

Around three in the afternoon, Luca received a frantic call from Celeste. It took a while for Tyson to calm her down enough to tell us what had happened.

From what Sheriff Veron had told her, someone had gone into Roots & Remedies and torn the place apart looking for something. Panic raced through me as she told us what had happened. Considering how upset Celeste was when she called, I knew she hadn't gotten to the bad part yet.

Aside from the shop being torn apart—likely someone searching for Hazel's spell book—Raymond was found DOA. Roslyn Keller, the lady who owned Stitched Up, next door to Roots & Remedies, was the one to report the incident. She'd heard stuff being thrown around the shop and knew it couldn't be Raymond.

My panic after hearing about the destruction had quadrupled. The man who was supposed to be having one of the most important conversations of the girls' lives with them was gone. It was up to us to deliver the packages Raymond had put together.

From what little Celeste had been told, the girls were safe but scared to death. Their parents would be arriving tomorrow to make the arrangements for Raymond. We knew Veron would have sent guards to the house, but we needed to get back to Salem. We had packages to deliver and two girls to protect.

Luca and I had experienced a lot of loss in our one hundred years, but this one would be by far the hardest. I wished we had met Raymond sooner. The past five years that we have been in his life were what made the days more bearable. The lives we lived were tough, but talking to Raymond and even hearing the stories of his adventures, seeing life through his eyes, made it worthwhile.

Chapter Thirteen

May 20, 2023

Luca

Colin and I received the first packages from Celeste that Raymond had put together for Sadie and Isadora. They consisted of two small boxes and one envelope.

We arrived at the door to Raymond's house on Franklin Drive. Veron had informed us that the girls were staying at his house until their parents arrived.

It was just after nine when I knocked on the door. Colin and I waited for one of the girls to answer. James, the security guard who worked for the GWP, stood on the other side of the small porch. He had been filled in on why we were there.

The door slowly opened, and Sadie stood in the doorway with Isadora a few steps behind. My gaze met Sadie's, and it was instant attraction. The photos Raymond had given us didn't do the girls justice. Sadie was much more beautiful and flawless in person, even with the messy bun and lack of makeup.

"Sadie Craig?" I asked, trying to keep my voice even.

She gave me a slow nod. "Yes, I'm Sadie," she said nervously.

I held out the small box with the envelope attached to it, and as she took it from my hands, her fingers brushed against mine. A spark ignited between us.

Colin straightened from the doorframe where he leaned. "Isadora Monroe?"

"Yes," she said, her voice strong.

He reached out and handed her the box.

"We will be back in ten days," I said as I broke the connection between me and Sadie by dropping my gaze.

We turned to walk away, and once we were past the corner of the house, I turned to Colin. "This may be the last binding we ever do. I hope it doesn't end in a reversal."

Colin looked back toward the house. "I have to agree with you on that one, Matthews. They are much more than I expected."

Sneak Peek

A Spell to Bind

Book One of The Green Witch Project Series

Chapter One

May 18, 2023

Sadie

I drove past a sign that said I was fifteen miles from Salem and turned the radio down to dial Izzy.

She picked up on the first ring. "Hey, Sadie!"

"So, are you ready for a summer full of training to become a Green Witch like Pops?" I asked, my voice full of excitement.

"You know it. I just wish I knew what all was involved," Izzy replied.

I rolled my eyes as I sensed the hesitation in her voice. "You worry too much. It'll be fun. What time will you get to Salem tomorrow? Pops should be at the shop until six, so we can grab a bite to eat when you arrive."

As I neared the exit to Amsterdam, a truck raced up the on-ramp, so I moved into the far-left lane. As I approached the place to merge, the truck cut across both lanes of traffic and slipped in right ahead of me.

I slammed on my brakes and jabbed my horn as I went around him. "Watch it, you stupid idiot," I growled. "Sorry, Izzy. People can't drive."

"Um, no, they can't." She chuckled. "Anyway, I'll probably be there about noon or so. I plan on leaving around nine. I'm packing a snack and eating breakfast before I leave, so I won't need to stop for food. But you know me. I'll probably have to pee, so let's go with twelve thirty or quarter to one at the latest."

"Ha ha. Yes, *Isadora*." I was one of the few people she let call her by her full name. "You will definitely need to stop to pee. So do you want to meet me at Veron's Sub Shop across from the car rental place? What time do you need to return the car?"

"No later than two. Are we sticking with last night's plan?"

"Sounds good to me. Text me when you leave in the morning. Good luck with your final exam this afternoon. You've got this." I looked in my rearview mirror for the idiot who had cut me off.

"Thanks, Sadie. Be careful on the rest of your drive. I'll see you tomorrow. Please do some of your breathing exercises before you see Pops. Love you."

"Love you too." I hung up and looked at myself in the rearview mirror. I needed to figure out Izzy's secret to staying so calm all the time. She would have just slowed down and given a little grunt about that man pulling out in front of her.

As I drove into Salem, I rolled down the windows and took a deep breath. The sun glared from behind the traffic light, warming my skin. I had spent the entire week inside studying for exams, so I figured a nice walk in the fresh air would do me some good. I drove to Pops's house, parked my car, and headed down Franklin Drive on foot.

As I turned onto Chester Street, I spotted a little gray squirrel at the base of the tree in Ms. Jones's front yard. By the time I reached the tree, he had disappeared into the top of it. I shielded my eyes from the sun and peered up into the branches.

A small voice came from nearby. Startled, I spun around. I didn't see anyone. I couldn't hear what had been said anyway. I picked up the few small branches from the sidewalk that had fallen from the old oak tree and laid them by the trash can at the curb. I looked around again before I gave a little shrug and kept walking.

As I turned onto Main Street, I caught the sweetest whiff of tomato and stopped dead in my tracks. I stood in front of a restaurant that I didn't remember seeing the last time I visited. A grumble rose from the depths of my stomach. I hadn't eaten since before I left Richmond.

The tables at the front of the bistro-style restaurant were empty, but a man stood at the register. I walked up, placed my order, and sat to wait. I was headed back out the door a few minutes later.

I continued down Main Street and peeked into the shop window at Roots & Remedies. I noticed a customer standing at the counter, so I waited for him to leave before going inside. When I was a child, Pops always said that the customers deserved his full attention while they told him what they needed. Because of that, I had never disturbed him while he was working, and I wasn't about to start.

I leaned against the side of the building and thought about how excited I was to spend the entire summer with Pops. I felt much calmer when I was around him. Growing up, Izzy and I had only been allowed to stay a week at a time. I didn't have a clue what she and I would be doing, but if I was with Pops, it didn't matter. He was my grandfather, but he had taken Izzy in and treated her as if she was his granddaughter as well.

As I shuffled a pebble around with the toe of my shoe, I remembered Pops telling me about how they had transformed the cobblestone part of Main Street into a walking mall back in the late 1950s. I had many memories of strolling up and down those lanes as a child. Pops always said the four-hundred-year-old roads were his favorite thing about Main Street.

I snapped out of my thoughts when I heard the jingle of the bell that sat over the door of Roots & Remedies. I peeked around the corner and watched as the customer exited the shop. A chill rolled over me as he walked past, and I hurried inside.

Pops had his back to me when I walked in.

"I'll be right with you," he said as he finished folding a piece of paper and tucking it into the back pocket of his pants. He wore the suspenders I got him last Christmas over a white T-shirt with jeans.

The shelves that wrapped the outside of the room were fairly empty of remedies, which was very odd. Pops always restocked as he sold things.

I tiptoed up to the counter. "Could you recommend any teas for me to purchase to celebrate completing another semester of college?"

Pops stopped what he was doing and slowly turned. His smile was there, but he seemed drained of color. "Oh, Rosebud, I am so glad to see you. I missed you so much." He reached up to brush back his loose white hairs then straightened and came out from behind the counter with his arms out.

I put the food on the counter and gave him a big hug. The scent of spice and mint filled my nose, and in that very moment, I was home. "I missed you, too, Pops. Are you okay?"

He stepped back, looking me over, his hands warm on my shoulders, and he gave me a small smile. "I'm okay. I had a tough request from a customer a few minutes ago. I'm worried I can't help him." He glanced at the door then back at me. "Where's Daisy?"

"Oh, she's coming up tomorrow. Her art class required her to take her final exam on campus, and she wasn't sure how long it would take. So I came by myself." I tilted my head a bit as I gauged his reaction.

His worried expression dimmed as he spotted the bag on the counter. "Whatcha got there, Rosebud?"

I wanted to ask him more about the customer request, but I knew Pops. He wouldn't share the situation with anyone until he came up with a solution. "I thought I'd surprise you with lunch. It's spaghetti from that new restaurant, Tastes of Italian."

"Oh, you surely know the way to a man's heart... and stomach." He pulled me into another hug and held it longer than the first one. "Go ahead into the kitchen, and I'll close the shop for lunch. I'll be right behind you."

As I walked from the front of the shop through the door to the kitchen, I noticed jars scattered across the countertops and mail covering the table. I removed the newspapers and piled the mail on the counter. Pops grabbed some sodas from the fridge and sat as I took our lunch from the bag. I handed him his silverware and napkins before settling into a chair.

I had never seen the shop so messy or Pops so beside himself in all the times I'd visited. My heart hurt for him. "Can I help you with anything today? Maybe something you need done so you can focus on the request."

Pops shrugged as he chewed the first bite. "I would love to work without having to stop each time a customer comes in. If you could help the customers, that would be great. I'd like to get this request completed as quickly as possible." He took a bite of his garlic bread and looked up at me. "This spaghetti is really gonna hit the spot. Thank you, Rosebud."

"You're welcome."

We sat in silence for the entire meal. I glanced at Pops every chance I got without being noticed. The worry lines on his face had deepened, and he looked tired. Pops seemed to have aged ten years since we visited for spring break. The normal twinkle in his eyes was overshadowed with worry.

Pops cleaned up his tray, tossed it in the trash, and finished his soda. "I'm going to get started on this project, if that's okay." He kissed the top of my head. "I'd like to work at the table in the greenhouse, where it's quieter, but just poke your head around the corner if you need me."

"Of course, and I'm here if you need to bounce ideas off someone or want me to research anything."

Pops smiled and went to the front counter to get his journal, messenger bag, and some loose papers from his desk beside the register. He walked by me to the greenhouse without another word, as if I weren't even sitting there. I wished I hadn't waited for the customer to leave before entering. Maybe I could have heard the request and tried to help.

I cleaned the kitchen and restocked what I could before I locked the door and turned off the Open sign and lights, then I peeked into the greenhouse. Pops wrote in his journal and referred to a sheet of paper that looked to be old and crumpled. "Hey, Pops, you ready to go home?"

"Huh?" He looked at his watch, and his eyes widened. "Oh my. I was so busy working that I didn't realize the time. Did you lock up?"

"Yep. You only had two sales this afternoon, dried sage and salve for poison ivy."

"Oh, well, thank you, Rosebud. I'll be ready in a moment."

He put his journal, papers, and pen in his bag and zipped it. We walked out the back door, and he locked it.

We got to the end of the alley before I broke the silence. "Did you get anywhere on your project?"

"I'm afraid not. I've narrowed down everything that won't work, though."

We stopped at the corner of Chester Street to wait for a passing car.

"Well, at least you got that part out of the way." I nudged his arm with my shoulder and gave a little chuckle. "Finding out what doesn't work is always part of solving things. It wouldn't be as rewarding if everyone got everything right on the first try."

Pops shot me a surprised look, and his fluffy white eyebrows twitched briefly. "You are too wise for your age, Rosebud. I have no doubts you will take over the shop when I'm gone." He took a deep breath and released a heavy sigh. "You know I won't be around forever."

I stopped walking, and Pops paused a couple of steps ahead before he turned around. He must have seen the tears forming in my eyes because he wrapped me in a hug.

I squeezed him tight, fighting the tears. "Pops, why would you say that?"

He squeezed me harder before pulling away and looking down at me. He wiped the tear that snuck down my cheek. "I'm no spring chicken anymore." He tucked his fingertips under his armpits and pretended to be an old chicken hobbling around. Pops always knew how to cheer me up.

"Oh, Pops. Stop that before someone sees you. They will think you've gone crazy if you cluck like that." I pretended to block my face so no one could recognize me.

He stopped and looked at me as if I had insulted him, and I couldn't help but giggle.

Pops smiled big for the first time since I'd gotten to town. "Oh, Rosebud."

He held out his arm. I wrapped mine around his, and we started walking down Chester Street toward his house.

Once inside, he hung his keys on the hook and walked into the kitchen. He opened the fridge and stared. "I don't have much here."

"That's okay. I'm not that hungry." I couldn't have eaten again anyway after that big lunch.

"Well, we still need groceries. My tablet thingy is on the dining room table. You can place a grocery order for delivery tomorrow. Go crazy." He rubbed his stomach. "I think I'll skip dinner tonight too. I'm still full from lunch. Italian food always fills me up too much, but it's so hard not to eat it all at once."

I rubbed my belly and nodded. "I do the same thing every time. I'll place an order for groceries and head to Dad's room if you need me. I'm sure you want to keep working on your project."

Pops smiled and kissed the top of my head then went back to his office.

Just like the kitchen in his shop, the dining room table was full of unopened mail, newspapers, empty glasses, and a plate. I took the dishes to the kitchen and noticed the sink was full of dirty ones. The mess might not be unusual at my home, but Pops never left his kitchen like that. I suppressed my building worry and started cleaning up for him.

I unpacked my bags and put on my pajamas. I pulled down the comforter, got settled, and opened my book. I went back a chapter since I hadn't read for at least two weeks. Before I knew it, I was picturing myself in Africa trying to track down an injured black panther. I loved books I could escape into like that.

Ding-dong, ding-dong.

Um, I'm in the middle of an African safari. Why do I hear a doorbell?

I jerked myself awake and sat up in the bed, removing the slumped book from my chest. It took me a minute to remember where I was and the previous day's events. As the memories flooded in, the doorbell rang again. I must have fallen asleep reading.

I jumped up and headed out of my room and down the hallway. I glanced at the stove clock as I passed the kitchen doorway. It was eight thirty in the morning. *Who's here this early?*

I opened the front door and looked around. No one was there aside from two cats, a gray one and a black one, walking down the sidewalk.

I guess I'm hearing things now. I backed up and started to close the door when something caught my eye to the right of the threshold. I pulled the door back open and stepped out onto the mat. I'd forgotten I ordered groceries the previous night. *Why am I so out of it this morning?*

I put the groceries away, and as I headed down the hall toward my room, I saw a yellow sticky note on the door.

Rosebud, I had to head out early this morning, but I'll see you this afternoon when Daisy gets to town. I love you both. XO.

I put the sticky note on my desk, took a shower, and piddled around until Izzy arrived.

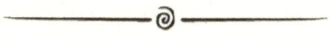

Izzy arrived right after lunch. She wore a pink tank top, light-blue jean shorts, and a pair of pink flip-flops. She pulled her long strawberry-blond braid over her shoulder.

Growing up, we had always been told that we could pass as sisters. We were both five foot seven and thin with long hair and freckles. Aside from Izzy's hair being blond and straight and mine being auburn and wavy, I had to agree.

"Hey, Izzy. How was your drive?" I stood and gave her a hug when she got to the table.

"It was okay. I only had to stop once to pee, so I think I made decent time."

"Well, I'm glad you're here. Pops will be so excited to see you. I wonder what he has planned for us this summer. We shouldn't have too much to learn before we can take over the shop and let him retire." I glanced up as we approached the oak tree where I had seen the squirrel the day before.

"Maybe he'll show us the banking and taxes. The book he gave me for my eighteenth birthday contains a list of every gemstone and crystal along with their uses, so I doubt I need to know anything else about them." She shrugged. "It's hard to tell with Pops. He's always full of surprises."

We had almost made it to the intersection of Chester and Main Street when a police car with flashing blue lights rounded the corner. It came squealing to a halt about a second after turning.

Izzy and I looked at each other then took off running. We turned the corner onto Main Street and stopped dead in our tracks. Four police cars and an ambulance sat in front of Roots & Remedies. Several officers came and went from the shop. We hadn't heard any sirens as we walked, and it looked as if they had been there for a while, but there was no sign of Pops.

We ran up to the building, but a police officer stopped us about six feet from the door. I tried to get past him, but he grabbed me and wouldn't let go. Izzy tried to walk farther, but another officer grabbed her.

"I'm sorry, ma'am. I can't let anyone in there. It's an active crime scene," the officer said as he tried guiding me back.

"Please, let me go." My voice came out a lot quieter than I wanted.

I tried to wiggle free, but the officer pulled me back.

"*Pops!*"

Acknowledgements

I would like to thank all my family and friends who have dealt with my book talk and read snippets. Thank you to Marissa and Amanda for doing the beta reads for me. Also, a huge thank you to my editors, Lynn, Amanda, and Virge at Red Adept Editing, for helping me through my journey.

A huge thank you goes out to Painted Wings Publishing as well. They did an amazing job on the edges for my special edition of this series as well as the chapter image. If you ordered my book from my website, the paper that was wrapped around the book was also designed by them. They are definitely worth working with, and I look forward to doing my next series with them.

About the author

I can't believe I've published a third book. Although this book is more about Luca and Colin, I hoping to give you some of the backstory that makes them a perfect match for Sadie and Izzy. Writing Sadie and Izzy's journey has been such an exciting experience. I'm so glad to have my readers joining them.

I have a son from my first marriage and a daughter and two stepsons with my husband. We have four cats and lots of local wildlife that surround us every day. I have incorporated some of the wildlife into this book along with some of our cats, one of which passed away as I began this adventure. Some of my characters are named after close family and friends as well.

I hope this series is one you will enjoy following these girls through. I have definitely enjoyed writing their story.

You can find me on the following social media platforms, through email, and website:

Facebook: Stacy Rae-Author

TikTok: @stacyrae_author

Email me at: stacyrae.author@gmail.com

Website: www.stacyrae-author.com

Also by

All of the artwork in this version of Demon in the Rift was drawn by Stacy in Procreate.

Keep a look out in 2025 for the following new titles.

A Spell to Bind- Book One of The Green Witch Project Series

Demon in the Rift- Book Two of *The Green Witch Project Series*

Broken Blood Spell- Book Three of The Green Witch Project Series

Evil Innocence- Book One of the Dreamer's Innocence Series